FLASHING THE SQUARE

microfiction and prose poems

edited by

Linda Godfrey
and Bronwyn Mehan

SPINELESS WONDERS
www.shortaustralianstories.com.au

Spineless Wonders

PO Box 220

STRAWBERRY HILLS

New South Wales, Australia, 2012

www.shortaustralianstories.com.au

First published by Spineless Wonders 2014

Cover image and design by Richard Holt

Edited and copyediited with the assistance of Laura Di Iorio. Layout by Bronwyn
Mehan.

Typeset in Franklin Gothic Book
Printed and bound by Lightning Source Australia
ISBN

Catalogue-in-print
A823.4
Flashing the Square prose poems and microfiction/
Godfrey, Linda & Mehan, Bronwyn (eds)

General observations   p. 63, 73,

Common them = city life   23, 27, 29, 45, 47

Australia

FLASHING THE SQUARE

microfiction and prose poems

Australian Government

This project has been assisted by the Australian Government through the Australia Council, its arts funding and advisory body.

'Why take 500 pages to develop an idea whose oral demonstration fits into a few minutes?'

JORGE LUIS BORGES,
Labyrinths

Contents

MARK SMITH

BIOGRAPHIES

EDITORS

THE JOANNE BURNS AWARD

Introduction

Some writers love a constraint. It sets their imagination racing. In this anthology we constrained our contributors' creativity, literally, into boxes. One box is a screen high above Melbourne's Federation Square, another the printed page and another inside your mp3 player. Whether these authors usually write flashpoint line poetry or prose, we asked for lines that ran from one margin of the page to the other. We were looking for writing which had the precision of poetry, for language that was brimful of suggestion and nuance. From inside the box, to outside the box, as it were.

Two hundred words maximum is all these writers were allowed. They gave us service station hold-ups, random violence in elevators, shark attacks and road fatalities. Complete narratives, with well-drawn characters and plot in less than a page. Here are short pieces about supermarkets, computers and dogfights – each packing an emotional punch. Here are quiet but no less significant moments: a child colouring in, a seagull stealing a chip. Writers showed us magic in the mundane of quotidian life – on trains, buses and trams and in backyard gardens and on nature strips. We gave them a blank square of paper to fill. They flashed it with political satire, memorable lines, mordant observations, flights of fancy and heartbreaking descriptions.

There has been debate recently about the 'problem' of how to read short short fiction. It asks whether you can read literature in a flash: on the go in your busy life, maybe on the ceiling while you are sitting in the dentist chair, taking in a quick literary experience as you multitask your way through the day. Or is it better to sit and savour the words, the language, the plot twists and the characters? Really immerse yourself in the experience. Let's call this 'the slow reading movement'. Here we offer all kinds of interactive experiences: you can sit with the book and take it all in, you can watch the pieces flashing on the screen as you walk through Federation Square, you can listen to them through your earbuds, you can watch and listen to the authors on screen on our website. In fact, you could do any and all of these when the mood grabs you.

This book is the result of a number of artistic collaborations. It is the companion publication for *Flashing The Square,* the video screening event designed and organised by artist, Richard Holt. Over a dozen contributions were flashed onto the large screens at Federation Square for the enjoyment of CBD passersby during the 2014 Melbourne Writers Festival. This anthology also brings together the work of invited writers and those hand-picked by microfiction afficiandos, Angela Meyer and Richard Holt, the 2014 judges of the *joanne burns* Award. As well, this book is accompanied by audio recordings made available during the Melbourne Writers Festival via a mobile app and to audiences everywhere via CD and mp3.

Spineless Wonders is proud to publish this unique book and to take part in the ground-breaking audio and visual microliterature experience. The editors would like to thank joanne burns, this year's judges and all of the contributors – our microliterati. Much applause to the dynamic and talented Richard Holt. Special thanks go to Laura Di Iorio for her editorial assistance and contributor wrangling. And thanks also to Melita Rien who managed the audio project.

Bronwyn Mehan
Linda Godfrey
2014

Susan McCreery

HOLD-UP

Rain scuds the late-night servo. A van in a parking bay, bearded driver asleep. A car at a pump. In the shop, Mrs Mac's pies sit in the warming box. A man in a hoodie thumbs through girlie mags under the white light. As the car leaves the pump, he fronts the counter. The attendant's palms rise. Empty the till, says the hoodie, waving his pistol. Okay, says the attendant. It's not. Is it? Davo? Morton Primary? Shut up and give me the money. Okay, says the attendant. I remember now. Fish paste sandwiches. When I didn' bring me lunch, ya'd share. Ya had the best sandwiches. Meanwhile, the van driver wakes, rakes his beard. Climbs down and heads for the glass doors. At the sight of the gun he backs off. Whattaya need it for, Davo? the attendant is saying. Ya hungry? I can give ya a pie. Take a pie, Davo. Go on. As the van driver pulls out his phone his hi-vis vest gleams. It catches the hoodie's eye.

— open-ended

— suspense/tense mood

— plays w/ the punctuation — no "." or " "

— sentence fragments → urgent — getting flashes of a scene

o list of commands

Kirsten Tranter

TURING TEST STUDY GUIDE

— title is important for story to make sense [handwritten]

computers can't act like humans - irony [handwritten, right margin]

paradox [handwritten]

Sweat. Don't sweat. Try too hard to relax. Forget your robot friends, their lilting gait. Wrack brains for that quotation from *Romeo and Juliet* to add to your response to question 5; just leave it. Revert to even more citationality. That is not what computers do. Make a pentameter by accident while claiming that you are not writing verse. Hide your machine heart, broken, present a bouquet to the judge.

paradox [handwritten]

Study. Don't study. Be yourself, don't think of who you were this morning, or how strange your feet seemed when seen in a strange bathtub. Suppress that nervous laugh, or at least leave it out of the teletype. Remember the apt quotation from the Sonnets, but get it wrong, just; you will seem less intelligent, but more human. That is the aim of it. Don't claim the sky is blue beyond compare. That is just the impossibility trope. Come up with something more original. Bare your analog soul, machine heart, broken, roses tattooed down the arm.

✳ What does it mean to be human? [handwritten]

23

✳ Telling a computer how to be human [handwritten]

Daniel John Pilkington

TRAM 96 TO ST KILDA

fragments

Corners. Jolting. Shoulders, elbows, knees, bags and flat faces, various tablets with their soft illuminations, their persistent genii. In the movement, we're one body, apologies unnecessary. Each of us is free to indulge in solipsisms or heavy-bearded rhythms, whether hanging from the plastic yellows or slouching across lurid greens. But this being a small world in itself, there is an exception. Two skinny brothers, knees knocking mine, bubbly and no doubt sugared for the afternoon, have decided to try on the contortions of a more mature anger, of which no parent could divine the antecedents. And so it begins. One simply refuses: *to have a conversation.* The other seethes: *you wouldn't know if you were having a conversation.* And the first, triumphant in closing some esoteric syllogism, nods: *a conversation is when someone hurts someone.* Silence. I see some mothers share knowing smiles, knowing how such smiles work. The boys have rather stunned themselves. Someone chuckles to no one and then the tram rings its bell and everyone leans in one direction. And, as this human carriage springs back into its equilibrium state, I stare out at that blazing smile stretching the face of the old funhouse.

the unspoken rules/interactions when riding on a tram

Hilary Hewitt

NO

raining

the bus is full   windscreen wipers, wet jackets   the woman
in front of you is wagging her head   continually   as if she is
saying yes yes yes yes   or no no no no   or even yes no yes
no in some mad morse code   but to whom   no earphones
the girl beside her texting not talking   the shaking speeds
up   pearl studs grey pixie crop   not the engine or we'd all be
vibrating   (you're feeling young today – christmas shopping,
the swarovski tree)   a silver bauble on a spring   tourette's,
you're thinking, poor woman   or parkinson's   a little shaken
about your future you look through that mesh that divides the
glass into tears of light   gutters overflowing umbrellas blown
inside out   this rain from typhoon haiyan   thousands suspected
dead   more asylum seekers washed overboard   operation
sovereign borders to protect against illegals   tropical storms
to grow stronger with global warming   the abbott government
not attending climate change talks in warsaw   you shake your
head   you can't stop

— repetition

light-hearted

— shift

serious
serious issues

— no capitalization or punctuation
— stream of consciousness – the
          randomness of our
                              thoughts
     >ADD
— rainy day – shows, not tells

Mark Roberts

CITY CIRCLE ?

you close your eyes & hear the rats in the ceiling. they have always been there waiting for the tunnel. after the last train they will take you there. they have their own poetry which you wouldn't understand & they have already written your epitaph. you know that they will make their home in your bones.

- no capitalization
- 2nd person
- theme = death
- unsettling - entretenido, provoca emociones, breve, cuenta una historia
  Swartwood ✓

Alana Hicks

MOVEMENTS

imagery — sounds

fragments

Three woman walkers - I'll put some towels out, people will want to swim in the pool. Man sitting angry - It's your money, do what you bloody well want with it. Traveling lady – her suitcase bumps along the broken brick. Recording bicycle man - swishes past with a camera helmet. His perspective of me catches mine of his. Woman gesticulating - emits loud "Caw" sounds as she flaps her arms about her head in heights of storytelling. Woman striding - Gunshot heels, measured, paced. Posture. Dead. Straight. Dude - Man of accumulated ages, fine with it, rolls by on skateboard stopping abruptly at the inevitable stairs.

clever

onomatopoeia

sounds

The Jackhammer. The Car Alarm. The Feather falls from a tree and floats backwards towards an indifferent sky. Nostrils burn with the overload. Cold wind and warm sun fight for domi-nance. Approaching Work, connections cease, recalling all that fills its walls. The faraway sounds of laughter. The printer, the elevator. Noises that echo in my every day, bounce around in an empty chamber. I look to my level above, look to my feet. Left. Right. This world is more than sights and sounds and smells, it's more than that, and it's less.

smell

feeling — touch

personification

main point ↑

31

Christopher Ringrose

WHITE OUT

I would have said 'I'm not enjoying this. Can we go home?' A million people to speak to, but no voice: my first night in Melbourne, with the smell of Shanghai in my clothes and airline food in my gut. 'It's White Night, you have to go into the city.' My socks were still rolled in my suitcase, eating each other neatly. I was on a tram track – a crowd atom, squeezed and stationary at the junction of Swanston and Flinders. I looked down at my small black pumps below my white ankles. Others' feet pointed in many directions; some trying to shuffle. Above, the skeletal blocks of the Square, the bank buildings and the station flickered orange and red, plastered with parodies of famous buildings or slow discos. Ahead and to the side, only the chests, arms, breasts and backs of people more cheerful than me. I heard their hum and mutter and was sucked into them. No motion has she now, no force. I vanished into a space that someone else immediately filled.

Joshua Maule

GIVEN

In the caravan's annex, he tapped the keys of his age-old laptop: drumming out thoughts from the year. They played fast, like slot cars, whizzing. The corners of his affections curled. Dedicated as he was to the task upon him – a writing project, a would-be book – he wondered if time would go on permitting him to think so hard and for so long? He shooed the thought, breathing, 'Never mind that right now'. No one else was there except for the voices on the album he'd been given, which played like a film soundtrack. It made the whole thing more nostalgic, though the songs were unfamiliar. That morning he had taken photographs of empty caravans, bunting, sand on the road, empty beaches and everything else around the apocalyptic landscape that is a holiday park in late winter. Summer would not delay of course. He could imagine children swarming in, clutching oversized chalk and riding new bicycles, as their parents drank wine and low-carb beers in chairs. He thought about all that. The thoughts satisfied him as company. It was funny how imaginings, dependent clauses, even adjectives, could satisfy a man. It was all given.

– He finds company (an escape from loneliness) in writing.

– the grammar is perfect – polished

35

Michelle Wright

TAKEN

The afternoon he was taken, the rangers put up beach closure signs and the patrols began by sea and air. The lone witness had said it was a Great White. 'Big as a campervan,' he'd said.

The police officer introduced her to the man coordinating the search.

'So, you're the young man's ... ?'

'Mother,' she said, 'and his name's Josh.'

When they reopened the beach three days later, they warned her, as softly as they could, that there was little chance of finding body parts. 'We think the shark took everything,' they said. She looked straight into their faces, and though they tried, they couldn't look straight back. *emotions*

Four days after they set the drum lines, they called to say they'd caught it. She went down to the beach and waited. She wanted so much to hate it. She wanted to spit on it, to kick its oily flank, to spew her grief into its jaws. She'd demand to know why, of all the flesh and blood it could have taken, it had chosen hers to take.

But when at last she saw its face with its fearful, lifeless eyes, all she truly wanted was to stand and stare and weep.

sharks are just animals — can't hate them for following instincts

Madeleine Baud

FRITZ

I keep having this dream. I'm floating in the ocean. Like, way out in the ocean. There's no land in sight, not even on the horizon. I'm floating on my back, looking up at the sky, watching the clouds wander. When I lift my head and look past my feet, I can see a boat. Everyone I've ever met is on that boat, and I mean everyone. My parents, my old tennis coach, that barista with the tattoo on her knuckle. All of them. I wave, but nobody notices; except for a dog. My old dog, Fritz. He barks madly at me. I hated that dog. I'm pretty sure the feeling was mutual. He bit me more than once. *like a conversation*

Anyway, we're slowly drifting away from each other, the boat and I. Each time I lift my head, it's a little further away. Each time I look up, I give them a little wave. Each time I wave, nobody notices except that mean old dog. I know that I'm eventually going to look up and I won't be able to see the boat anymore. I know that when that happens, they will have forgotten me. Everyone but Fritz.

— dogs are more loyal than people?

sad — evoca emociones

Caroline Reid

ONE BLUE EYE

The dog at the BP in Fitzroy Crossing had one blue eye, a torn ear and a mind opened by the wound in the top of her head. Even Dave looked twice. And it takes a lot for Dave to react. On the dry grass verge behind the dog, a blue-heeler waited, uncertain of the outcome of the fight. Had he been won or not? And if so, why was she stalling? Balls twitching, lipstick out, he sniffed the air for a clue. The dog didn't move. *??*

A slow parade of muddy, four-wheel drives and camper vans steered clear of her. Grown ups and children rubber-necked to gawp at the dried blood dress, the one blue eye, the ten mile stare, the meaty crown. She wasn't moving. 'Tough bitch,' said Dave. 'You wanna coffee?' He parked away from the dog, giving her a wide berth on his trek to the roadhouse, just like everyone else. Her circle of stillness was sacred. Her place had teeth. She wasn't about to lick her wounds in public. *– alive*

– dog fight?
road kill – but is she dead?

maybe

Emily Clements

FOREST

imagery

From nascent darkness the moon hangs knife-like, razor point glistening with intent. Walk through air thick and cold as reptile blood, shadows pooling from the stab wounds of your one-two footfall. The night around you is a pack of wolves eating up the horizon, lupine devils devouring day's remnants of peach- *allit.* coloured sunlight. Wind slides slippery fingers to the back of your *person.* eyes and pulls tears, like wet curtains, down your cheeks. Heart kicks, wild rabbit fear bursting against bones in a body made of dust and memory. You pause beneath the trees with their leaves quivering tight as arrows to the string and realise you are deeper *simile* than you have ever been before, more lost than you have ever been before. Then, it's just you and me in the clearing; grass *2nd* crackles around our ankles and you're wearing that blue dress I *person* like. All I am and was and will be is laid out in silver moments by your soft hands. The wolves hang their black skins between the stars, my organs mash and grind together in bloody monstrosity, and you, you can see everything. Who knew a girl so small could swallow you whole with barely a pause in her prettiness.

— a guy likes this girl
+ they're in the
woods at night
— werewolf?

Irene Wilkie

THE LAST HARE

The hare's long ears stand and turn. Survival is his tutored game. Ginger-haired and the size of a poodle, he lopes silently out of the bushland reserve. Here, politically misplaced, he should not be growing fat on environmentally conserved and native grasses, should not be stealing sustenance from the mouths of wallabies, should not be seeking diversity in my rose garden. He watches me and listens and I let him have his rose. He knows I am no shooter or fox or dog. I know where his burrow dives under flat sandstone. He knows I know and would invite me there if I could fit. It's a secret between us. The other secret I know but will never tell him is that he is the last hare in this reserve. He has made friends with the wombat under my house and the possum in my roof and the echidna in my garden – and me.

He is content. My roses bloom each day. There are plenty for us both.

[handwritten annotations: environmental issues; – share w/ animals – be kind to them; – human connection with animals]

Katelin Farnsworth

SEAGULL

[handwritten: fragments   show, not tell]

Bleak sun. Curling waves. Short, stubby grass. Hands every-
where. Corn chips scattered. Guacamole unopened. A faded
picnic rug. *[handwritten: picnic on the beach]*

Seagull watching. Beady eyes. Flickering. Moving up and down.
Side to side. Stringy legs step carefully. Wings rustle, flap,
shiver in blue light, rain dances from the sky. Clear threads of
light. Silence. And then, running. Racing. Scooping the chip up.
Turning away, soft, white head shining.

He looks back. They are staring at him, his plush feathers worn
and weakened. They are standing, and laughing, curved fingers,
pointing as he makes his great escape.

He carries the corn chip in his mouth; letting saliva warm it up,
turn it soggy. He lifts himself up into the wind, stretches his
wings – his long, beautiful wings and glides. The chip dangles
from his mouth. He bites down on it and it falls. It collapses
into the sea. He watches it tumble, takes a gulp of stagnant air,
swoops and follows it. *[handwritten: imagery]*

*[handwritten: – a seagull steals a chip
– who knew you could
tell a story
about that?]*

Harriet Gaffney

SWAN SEASON

Swan season I called it.

We used to sit by the lake and watch the black swans, see how they shared responsibility for the nests and the young, how they flocked. She told me stories about the chips of stone she had found – axe heads, from the people long ago. Her eyes were far away as she talked.

Sometimes she'd tell me about the beginning, when Bunjil *folk tale* created the land and its features, how his wives, the black swans, looked down from the skies. I loved that story, although in my imagination I always changed it: watched the wives fly down from the heavens and coast over the flat lands, tilting their wings to draw the outline of the ridges, opening their beaks and trumpeting the lakes, creating wind with which to make the trees sing – leaving Bunjil up there with his rages and stern face, brewing the big storm.

Tim Sinclair

LISTEN

[handwritten: 2nd person]

[handwritten: command]

Listen. No. I mean, look. Watch this space. It's our final frontier, this something between us, and we have to come out to the edge of ourselves to shout across the chasm.

If you would only stand still for more than a second, I could ask about your troubles. You could tell me. Can't you give me a moment from your day, a grain of your existence? I need you. I'm not complete without you. If you close your eyes, I disappear.

I'm not quite sure how we got here. I didn't intend to be so far in debt to your focus. But there's something wistful about depend-ence, don't you think? Your attention cradles me like a hatchling under a heat lamp and I feel my feathers growing because of it.

You're going to help me fly. Don't turn away. I will circle your oceans until I'm sure of your existence and then spiral down to land in the palm of your certainty. Feather brush wingtip on the inside of your wrist. Don't be afraid. Your hands are steady.

[handwritten: Who is the speaker?]

[handwritten: confusing]

jenni nixon

PROPOSAL

marry me. please say yes. marry me. in our local church with a choir singing and church bells ringing. words we'll say in blessed matrimony: love honour. love graffiti on an overpass across the main road strung up for all to see scrawled upon a fluttering sign suspended high from the railway bridge. marry me. hired a skywriter his plane flew over our house the words written in white snow on blue sheets. you saw them smiled. i know your body like my own. the curves smells folds of it. the licks of tongues to fire passions breathe of it. though we share our bed you cannot be my wife. church forbidden. no white frocks gold rings wedding bells no rainbow confetti no battered shoes to knock the road behind a sign: just married. my love here is my proposal – when the law is changed – marry me.

gay marriage proposal

53

Shady Cosgrove

MY PAST IS SHOPPING AT WOOLWORTHS

[handwritten: –important]

[handwritten: in media res]

I'm trapped between the deodorant and shampoo, trying to deci-pher my wife's handwriting, while Joe – my two-year-old – stacks soap into an aisle fortress. I'm re-shelving the boxes when I hear my name, the second syllable a question. 'It's good to see you,' I manage, standing up.

It's been five years, maybe longer, and she's still so familiar. A few more creases around the eyes, a little thinner in the face. Joe is giggling behind me but we stand there until she asks how I am. She's rocking her trolley, says she's working at the same place. Mentions her colleagues, her mother (awkward laugh) and the whole time she's watching Joe like *that'd-be-right* and I'm thinking of her birthday in our tiny flat – over-baked lasagna and cheap wine, piles of baking soda on a ruined tablecloth and the door open, unslammed after she left.

[handwritten: – seeing an ex-at a common place – det at a grocery store]

[handwritten: –married]

Julie Chevalier

MARRIAGE OF CONVENIENCE

a small painting of marquis lodovico's daughter dorotea sent
from mantua by courier   to be inspected by her would-be
spanish groom   he'll check if her nonna's genes are tangled in
the gonzago laundry   (her younger sisters & their deformities
already packed off to convents)   despite cruel allegations &
medical examinations   sweet dorotea frescoed to the wall
asserts her capacity to strengthen alliances   & trade flesh to
breed heirs   the spaniard accuses her of being a hunchback
& weds the sister-in-law of the french king   — surprise ending

how shallow marriage
was back them
— it was political
— beauty prized

Ally Scale

I DO

Raymond ambles toward St Michael's Church to attend Clare and Charlie's wedding. He curves through the concentrated crowd and stumbles up the steps. Inside is a scene plagued by stiff-backed money, guests with buoyant hair sit rigidly in pews, smooth hands resting in their laps. I don't belong here, he thinks.

relatable

The organ clangs noisily around the hall and the guests stand to attention. The air is thick with anticipation. Clare winds down the aisle with a nervousness so stark it causes Raymond's heart to suck in and out like a concertina. Her 'I do' is docile; Clare is timid and unassuming. Raymond wonders what the two talk about when they come home from work each night. He wonders about that a lot. The pressure bubbles in his chest, filling his lungs with salted air. His head is clogged with memories of Charlie: of late night phone calls, of tussles in sand dunes, of Saturday nights soaked in liquor and lazy passion. These memories fade with each step the newly anointed couple make down the aisle.

Raymond lingers at the back of the church in the shadows, surrounded by a cluster of bodies, with his fists in tight balls.

gay man attends his ex-boyfriend's wedding to a woman

Angela Meyer

TO AND FROM YOUR HOUSE

It's not a suburb I know well. Butchers and bakers and a shop that sells wool. All closed at this hour. The suburb feels remote, but the sky has that tourmaline glow. Day for night.

Just a lamp on in your living room, and the pink-orange street-lights seeping in. My chest, too, feels aglow. You've never invited me so late. We watch a crime show on TV. 'I think about that so much, undressing the dead,' you say. I never have before, but now I do. It has to be someone's job, to peel or snip away a dress, sleeves, a pair of grey underpants.

We remove each other's clothes with a new quiet after that.

The outside is both pinker and greener when I go, early, to get ready for work. The people on the tram smell like dust.

Swartwood

- too long
- entertaining
- tell a story
- evokes emotion
- hints at miscarriage
- invita reflexión?

Valls

- ellipsis — don't know
- dynamismo   all that
- conciso ∅   happend
                 between
- ambigüidad   them
- poco humor

- in media res
- mixes the lights in — the ordinary

Theme

serious thoughts
in the ordinary
moments of life

Style

- in media res
- short sentences
  → quick
- circular — starts
  + ends w/
  light changing
- breveded represents
  mode of
  thinking

Susan McCreery

LIGHTS

[handwritten annotation: 3rd person — omniscient narrator]

[handwritten annotation: in media res]

Another red light. He palms his chin, taps the steering wheel. Sport-plus-shopping traffic. Next to him his wife is silent. What a way to spend Saturday morning, stuck in the car with her in a mood. His head hurts from last night. That's why she's pissed off. Green, but only two cars make it through. The hulking yellow and blue sign taunts in the distance. Bloody IKEA. He can't stand the place. Full of pregnant women nesting. Her mother coming from the UK and they have to set up Home Beautiful. Bed. Lamp. Side table. Even a rug. What's the point in her visiting now? She hasn't said a word since they left home. Neither will he. Play that game. Good at it. Coloured streamers on cars. Must be junior grand final. Rather be cheering on the sidelines instead of shopping. Makes a fist – small as this, he was. Small enough to fit in his hand. Their boy. Won't think about it. No one's fault. Don't think about it. Green. Slams on the accelerator. This time he'll make it through. *[handwritten: 181 words]*

[handwritten annotation: lol humor]

[handwritten annotation: miscarriage??]

[handwritten annotation: stream of consciousness thoughts]

[handwritten annotation: wife is pregnant & the baby is not wanted?]

[handwritten annotation: the serious intermingled w/ the ordinary of our lives]

Cameron Semmens

I SAW A MAN DIE

I saw a man die. Road rage. One punch. The old man toppled like a matchstick. His skull hit the road, his legs didn't move. From where I sat, eating pizza, I didn't see his head hit the ground, but I heard it. It was a slap ... of sorts. You'd think it would be a crunch, or a crack, but it wasn't. I cried out something in that moment, but I don't remember what. The guy who threw the punch just drove off. I got his number plate. I wrote it on the back of my hand.

'It's evidence', the cops said when they took a photo of the scrawled numbers on my sweaty skin. They also took a photo of the table I was sitting at, with me sitting there. I accidently smiled. The pizza I'd eaten was throwing itself around my stomach like it wanted to escape. The press were hawking; cameras were on me. It started to rain. An excuse to run, and run I did! A reporter chased me down the road. But I had no words for him, just a sound: a slap, a weird slap ... with a very long echo.

pers [handwritten annotation in left margin]

he died too? no. [handwritten annotation]

Shady Cosgrove

CALL AN AMBULANCE

The police said he was approached in an elevator by two
assailants. Not true. There were three of them – baggy t-shirts,
bandanas and hi-tops. They got on at the fifth floor, calling each
other names too crass for the middle of the afternoon. When
Patrick tried to step aside the one with the goatee nudged him
back. Something didn't feel right, of course it didn't, but the
doors were already closing. In his peripheral vision Patrick could
see the skinny one rubbing at his arms but kept his gaze trained
on the round plastic buttons – two of the numbers had been
scratched off – and just when the elevator got some traction,
just when Patrick thought he was being a paranoid dickhead,
the one with the bruised eye socket jammed a key into the panel
and they all shuddered to a halt.

Jon Steiner

TOOTH

He brushed his teeth before going to bed. He brushed them good and hard. He brushed them so hard, one of them fell out. He leaned on the sink, looking down at it. The sink came loose from the wall and crashed to the floor, crushing both his feet and gashing his ankle. He staggered into the hall and stepped in a bear trap, which snapped shut around his shin. After prying the bear trap open and extricating his leg, he hopped down the hall. He hopped through some broken bottles and tacks, causing him to fall sideways against the banister, which gave way and sent him tumbling down the staircase onto the floor in the hallway. As he lay there staring up at the hanging light fixture, it came loose from the ceiling and crashed down on his face, shattering into a million pieces and gouging out one of his eyes. He dragged himself back up the stairs, pushed open the bedroom door and crawled into bed next to the woman who hated him. She mumbled something and then rolled over. He lay in the dark and with his tongue felt the space where his tooth used to be.

Linda Godfrey

LUNCH

Bird shops till her money is gone. While walking home to Grandma's she eats grapes, bananas, takes the lid off the honey, dips her fingers in, scoops it to her mouth, drips it over the parcels, herself. Licks her forearms clean, opens sesame cakes. At home, she spreads tahini on a cut apple, drinks more from the jar. Fills a jug of water. Spills sunflower seeds on the floor. Scrabbles around, shoves them into her mouth with bread-crumbs and cat hairs.

Crawls to the toilet. Arranges herself over the bowl, fingers down her throat. Vomits. Wipes her mouth. Spits. A chunk of food caught up her nose. Spits again. Washes her mouth. Drops in Clear Eyes. Goes to her grandmother's bedroom, crying. In the dresser she finds the box with their Christmas savings. Port Douglas, the reef, do some diving, stay a night at the Mirage.

Bird heads to Smith Street. Buys beans, carrots, kale, oranges, lemons, bread, noodles, miso. Goes home. Hides most of it under her bed. She finds two bags of rotting apples there. Throws them out.

She leaves a note, Bought food for tea. I'll eat later.

Swartwood

- entertaining
- tells a story
- emotions

→ too long
* invita a reflexión

Valls

- final sorpresa
- no es elíptico o
                    conciso
- título es importante

Angie Holst

ADDICTED

1st person

How did I end up in rehab? — *starts w/ a question*

I couldn't sleep at night for the twitching, couldn't stop thinking about it. I would clench and unclench my fist over and over again. Clench, unclench; twitch. Without it, life was nothing. I had lost confidence in my ability to make simple decisions; I needed its affirmation, its bolstering. Going cold turkey left me a basket case: I couldn't concentrate at work, couldn't engage with friends, couldn't muster up the most basic of conversation. I felt alone: isolated without it. I was outside everything; I no longer felt part of the group. When I found myself awake at night, desperate for another hit and looking for the company of those night-owl friends, I knew I needed help.

They took it off me when I arrived at the clinic; shut me away in a room without any stimuli. They said I needed to get back to my old life; engage again with work, family and outdoor hobbies. But I just wanted one more hit. One more awesome tweet to get to five thousand followers. I missed the highs: like the day I was retweeted by Wil Anderson. I don't think I'll ever be that happy again. *almost 200 words*

— surprise ending — the addiction is social media

— modern issue

Dael Allison

ON THE WRONG SIDE

poetry

you got up this morning on the wrong side of the gong the wrong slide of the trombone the blocked end of the bugle out of step with the whole marching band. you got up this morning on the slip side of the scale the square side of the treble clef the slow side of capriccio your harmonium in delirium. you got up this morning on the minor side of major with falsetto in your bass a rumble in your trill cacophony in your homophony. you got up this morning with your up on a downbeat your score incomplete a tarantella in your a capella a tirade in your serenade. you got up this morning singing in a different key but baby you got up on the right side of me. yeah.

— no punctuation or capitals

— rhyme + rhythm

— music theme

— sound like a rap

Richard Holt

PARTICLE PHYSICS

My sister arrived, at last, at the Library of all Notions, in a
kingdom of peaks and low white cloud. Behind heavy doors,
in disappearing rows, were the volumes that held the knowl-
edge of the world. She went instinctively to the furthest corner.
Breathed the mustiness of time. Sunbeams played above the
shelves. As she reached for her answer she understood and it no
longer mattered that the book's only words—your search is your
purpose—turned to dust in the act of peeling back the velum.

Ruth Wyer

I DON'T USE MY POWERS FOR GOOD

in media res

I was 24 when I first stopped time. It was sheer anger that did brought it on. Stuck in a roasting tin can. Sardined between commuters clipping their nails, shouting into their phones, and blaring music from cheap earphones that suck in all the bass but leave the tinny treble and crappy lyrics to bore holes in my skull.

I don't use my powers for good. Why should I? We're each on our own in this world. Never more so than now. When I stop time I take the mobile phones from the shouters on the trains. I smash them against the handrails and place the phones back in their hands. I take the scissors from the nail cutters and use them to snip the earphone cords of music blarers. Sometimes I cut the ponytails or fringes of their owners. Just because I can.

No-one suspects me. When I restart time I'm feigning sleep against the grimy windows, swallowing the rising fear of the person I'm becoming, and of how these missing seconds must come back at some point – vengeful and unstoppable – to engulf us all.

Linda Godfrey

CHICKEN MANURE IS PERFUME

Jane arrives at the front gate, 'You know it smells really bad out here.'

To me, it smells of broody hens and freshly baked bread. 'I've spread chicken manure under the roses.' I say.

Jane wrinkles her nose.

I pick up a hen and bury my fingers deep in her warm and dusty feathers.

We go inside. I plonk the hen in the baby's high chair.

I've made rose sorbet. Chosen pale roses that hint of peaches and honey for flavor, and red-black ones for colour. Soaked out their fragrances and tints, composted the pale damp sludge of petals. Churned the liqueur into a vibrant, deep pink snow.

I feed it to my friend.

'It tastes like...roses!' she says. 'Beautiful.'

I smile at her with a mouth full of feathers.

Shady Cosgrove

LIGHTNING RIDGE

2ⁿᵈ person

It's a dirty, hot day so bright it feels like you need sunglasses, but you're already wearing them. We're playing Two-Up and everyone around us is wearing dusty thongs or work boots. The air is rough from beer. 'Heads!' you call and someone nods as the coins go up in the air, turning against the cloudless sky.

You left an inner-city terrace for this dirt town. You picked a plot, but like all of us, you're still hoping. Johnno found opal last year – next claim over – and you thought you could follow his seam, but the earth wasn't so generous. The coins land and you hand over the bills.

Jon Steiner

HOW TO INSTALL

A Sydney winter's day: deep blue sky, clouds drifting, sun gently warming the brick houses of an inner-west street, the kind with trees in the roadway, their middles pruned out to avoid power lines, cars parked between them. The verge's grass is radiant green thanks to the bountiful rains that precede winter and the gardens are dizzy with flowering shrubs. Except at one house, which features a sparse, well-kept lawn populated only by a few rose bushes pruned back severely for winter. On the kerb, between two parked cars, a bald man in his thirties, beard but no moustache, dark-blue shorts, light-blue work shirt, bare legs splayed out in front of him, peers intently down at a small, white booklet on the ground. In his hands, held up and off to one side so as not to obstruct his view of the booklet, is the cistern of a toilet, from which protrudes a small length of PVC pipe surmounted by a black O-ring. From the car to his left, a white Holden, comes a muffled radio sports report. A jet overhead lofts its way to somewhere in the distance. Somewhere far, no doubt.

everyday moment in the neighborhood

85

Barrie Walsh

CROSSING FRACTAL RIGHT ANGLE FLAGS

Hypotenuse seems obtuse, but so did *Griffith has malted the arrow-root*. *Bisk* abbreviates *biscuit*, acronyms *bacilloscopical index of skin*. Leprosy... *bisk* slang's what's left in underpants or between sheets.

BI alphanumeric squared 292=841 & 400+441 as 202+212 encodes TU=BI. As cities, TU placebo Timaru, between Christchurch & Dunedin; Timaru & Griffith acrostic T&G is *Tongue-&-Groove* housing method, symbolizes sex & lovemaking; MEL equates 132=52+122.
FED Square 62+52+42=77 is 20th Century Donald Mackay's 15 July 1977 murder. Melbourne & Griffith initials 13x7=91, being FED Square's hidden capstone 32+22+12=14+77=91.
A Tale of Two Cities as TV's *Underbelly* dramatized.
Now you see, now you don't, FED Square under sun & night-sky.

Southern Cross & pointers Alpha & Beta Centauri transcends equator. Amerigo Vespucci named 1501 rediscovery Almond, *vesica piscis* in Italian, America feminine of Amerigo, Waldseemuller's 1507 World Map accuracy of then unknown mystifies.
    ALMOND is L-MONAD as L=900 & MONAD Pythagorean God. Mason legends Solomon's Temple dig, 9 Knights Templar illiterate. Lambert of St Omer reads star *Merica* scrolls, latitude to sail west. BISK flees authorities; *on the lam*, Old Norse *lemja*, to lame, begets *beat it.*   *lemja* is 122+52=132 'one-o-one'

1901 Federation X factor SK=1911 as 21@91 is UIA;
Union International Architects/Astronomers: books pre-1501 *Incunabulum*. Sword of Orion, seven sisters Pleiades; what's up, goes down, a POV.

Richard Holt

FREE MARKET

This then was all that was left. Dex's climb had been strato-
spheric. At thirty he'd been ready to fly. Too close to the sun. The
crash hit hard. The auditors did their job for once. His bosses held
him to account for the same things they'd once demanded of
him. Everything disintegrated. Now this was all. A torn mattress,
a dirty blanket, a transistor radio and a bunch of clothes. Four
walls and a barred window. He kicked his belongings together
into a corner, sucked his last cigarette almost to the filter then
flicked the glowing butt into the pile. Black latex smoke started
curling upwards. It pooled beneath the ceiling. A lick of purple
flame struck up among his t-shirts and jeans. He glanced at the
door. Now at least he had options. Freedom of choice. That's
what made this country great.

[handwritten marginalia: "got caught 'n fraud"]

[handwritten note below text: "in prison he feels free – but ? before he was enslaved to climbing the corporate ladder"]

Cassandra Atherton

RUBBISH

in media res

It is Tuesday and I am dreaming that I live inside the trashcan on your computer screen. Bottom right. Lid slightly ajar. My head popping up at intervals to ask you why you left me. You have three reasons but I can't hear what they are. The trashcan graphic is too solid and sound waves ricochet off the crenulations. Facets. Indentations. You type your responses and drag them to me so I can read them. I wait for you in the trashcan. I wait for your mouse to lift me up and make me an icon. I want to shimmer and pulse so you recognise me. I want to be a square pink button with a harp sound when you click on me. I want you to constantly press on me. Double click. I want your mouse to slide over me. Tips of the fingers tapping out a morse code on the left click button. As I sit. Patiently. Singing *Kumbayah* and toasting pink marshmallows. Listening for you. You never let anyone else use your computer. No foreign fingers have touched the keys so I feel safe. Innocent. Virginal. I am yours. I am the only trashcan you have ever used. I wonder if you have been unfaithful. If you have used other computers when I am sleeping. If you prefer other trash cans. I worry every day that you will go to 'Empty Trash' and I will disappear.

personification of the trash can on your computer

Linda Cook

THE APPLE TREE

At the side of the shed, where the sun hardly ever reaches, a thick bed of moss stretches out towards the apple tree like a blanket, inviting Rosie to touch. Bare, curling toes help her spring up, the bark is smooth from a thousand earlier climbs, and the branches are solid and swaying.

The birds don't like it of course, but they can sod off, she's not hurting anyone, and the view over the side fence of the neighbours over grown forest helps her make believe it is long ago, or far away, or even once upon a time. The sun is warm, spattering her face and hands with light as the branches sway and the leaves dance, and the air smells of jasmine and eucalyptus.

Up in this tree she could be anyone, a rock star hiding from the paparazzi, a ghost already dead and gone: anything would be better than the truth; lonely, oddball girl of fifteen with a couple of drunks on welfare for parents, and a dead big brother. She sighs, resting her head back against the cool, fragrant bark, missing the blossoms of spring that have turned into stunted, blighted fruit.

— escape from reality
through her imagination

Karina Ko

GROWING UP

When I think of my mother through the eyes of my childhood, I think of the time our house was robbed, and she told us to wait in the car while she went inside by herself.

When I think of my father through the eyes of my childhood, I see my mother crying as she drove me home from school, asking if I found the lady in the photo beautiful.

When I think of my mother through the eyes of my adolescence, I think of the times she refused to turn down the television outside of my room, and how she yelled at me for crying.

When I think of my father through the eyes of my adolescence, I see a man eating like a goldfish, bits of wet food squelching against the insides of his mouth.

When I think of my mother now, I see a cocoon of blankets on the couch, watching television while playing games on her phone, and asking if I am free on the weekend.

When I think of my father now, I see a hunched grey man who leaves the dog bowl on the dining table, and frozen chicken on bits of newspaper.

Angela Smith

THE SPARE ROOM

Oars lapping the water, a rowing boat makes its way across the horizon. A woman in a red dress watches from shore, her skirt spinnakered by the wind. The woman's face is engraved with grief. A small girl squats on the sand, long black hair hooked behind her ears. She is busy with a stick writing her name in the sand.

This is the picture captured in the frame; this is the memory frozen in time.

A man hunches at a kitchen table in a circle of light thrown by a single globe. The man's past is stored in the spare room in a box of photographs of a woman with a red dress and a black-haired girl, smiling for the camera, smiling for her father who sits at the kitchen table in a circle of light, remembering.

A.S. Patrić

HB

The two women were speaking half-turned toward each other on the couch while the boy sat at their feet on the carpet. He had a clean sheet of paper and two grey lead pencils, just sharpened for him by the woman wearing black. He had followed her to the kitchen and had watched her sharpen the pencils over the sink with a butcher's knife. The pencils pierced the unruled piece of paper on the carpet. She'd been wearing black for years because of a dead son. Living alone now. He wondered how old the boy had been.

The first time he and his mother visited had been brief. This time the two women settled in to talk about writing. Both had been writers in another language and in another country. She wasn't old—the boy had seen crones before who always wore black. No wrinkles on the back of her hands and her fingernails were perfect and clear. He'd noticed when she gave him the two grey leads in the kitchen. When she patted his hands. His mother's fingernails broke easily, one or another often cut to the quick, and they were always painted red.

Ali Jane Smith

SANS RELACHE

What to do when you wake up feeling like a character from Balzac? Life teems around you, you, you, an emblem of your time. One day you're a bit player, the next agonist, liable to admire or detest yourself on the next page, in the next paragraph, by the end of this sentence! You have at last escaped the torpid countryside, but a reversal of fortune or a long explanation of thieves' argot could arrive without notice. At any moment you might forever disappear from the narrative. And all the time the scent and stink of Paris in your nostrils, as you walk your kids to the bus stop, buy milk and bread, ignore the newspaper, clutch for the phone settled deep in your handbag, alors, now what?

Mark Smith

THE METEOROLOGIST'S DAUGHTER

At birth, Penelope's skin bore the faint imprint of a weather chart. As she grew, the pigment darkened revealing a high-pressure cell centred over her stomach. A cold front hovered on her right thigh and a deep low, its isobars packed tightly together, covered her back.

On her eighteenth birthday, the pattern started to move, each day a little more. Her life took on meaning as she watched her skin for signs of trouble.

She issued sheep graziers' alerts when she was woken with premonitions of innocents caught out in the weather, their little bodies still covered in the liquor of birth. Boats pulled from their moorings, skiers lost in mountain blizzards and school picnics forced indoors, she bore responsibility for them all.

At twenty, she slept with Jacob, their bodies pushing tightly against each other in the night. In the morning, lying with their shoulders touching, Penelope saw that the isobars rising and falling over her breasts now looped onto Jacob's shoulder and across his chest. They shared a high-pressure system.

There was not a breath of wind.

She smiled, turned to him and held his body against hers.

'Good morning, Sunshine,' she whispered.

Biographies

DAEL ALLISON is a writer and editor. She won the 2012 Henry Kendall Poetry Award and the 2010 Varuna/Picaro Press Award. Her volume of poetry, *Fairweather's Raft*, was published in 2012 by Walleah Press. Dael currently lives in Kiribati.

CASSANDRA ATHERTON is a writer and critic. She has written a book of poetry, *After Lolita* (Ahadada Press, Tokyo and Toronto, 2010); a novel, *The Man Jar* (Printed Matter Press, New York and Tokyo, 2010) and her prose poems have recently appeared in *Best Australian Poems 2012* and *2013*.

MADELEINE BAUD is a designer who writes, a writer who illustrates, an illustrator who is pretty handy with a camera and a photographer who is really, really, really bad at maths.

JULIE CHEVALIER writes poetry and short fiction in Sydney. Her third book, *Darger: his girls* (Puncher & Wattmann) won the Alec Bolton Prize. It was short-listed for the WA Premier's Poetry Prize, 2013. juliechevalier.net

EMILY CLEMENTS is an emerging writer with a passion for nature and travel. She has recently returned to Australia after working as an editor and journalist in Vietnam. She currently studies writing and editing at RMIT.

LINDA COOK is a mum, a wife, a daughter, a sister, and a writer. Her stories, she says, are like her children; all unique and hard to let go of, but always with you, no matter what.

SHADY COSGROVE is the author of *What the Ground Can't Hold* (Picador, 2013) and *She Played Elvis* (Allen and Unwin, 2009), which was shortlisted for the Australian Vogel Award. She teaches creative writing at the University of Wollongong.

KATELIN FARNSWORTH is currently studying Professional Writing and Editing in Melbourne. She has been published in *Voiceworks* and shortlisted in the Rachel Funari prize for fiction 2014. She dreams of endless libraries.

HARRIET GAFFNEY won the 2012 Grace Marion Wilson Award for Creative Non Fiction. She has been obsessing about white relationship to place since her return to Victoria in 2011, after almost twenty years away.

HILARY HEWITT works as a building designer and heritage consultant in Sydney's inner west. She is currently completing her first novel which was shortlisted for the 2012 HarperCollins Varuna Awards for Manuscript Development.

ALANA HICKS is a writer, performer and director. She has performed with collective's *Token Word*, *Outspoken*, *Word Travels* and had writing featured as part of the National Play Festival, Sydney Festival, Sydney Writers Festival and more.

ANGIE HOLST is a Sydney based writer. Her YA novel *Expectations* was published in 2013 by Really Blue Books.

RICHARD HOLT coordinates *Flashing the Square*, a microfiction video project for public screens. He writes microfiction, poetry and longer form fiction and blogs about microfiction (bigstorys-mall.com). He was a cofounder of the zine store, *Sticky*.

KARINA KO is a twenty-something girl from Sydney who is slowly self-learning how to write well. She is particularly interested in poetry and short fiction at the moment.

SUSAN MCCREERY is a short story writer, poet and proofreader from Thirroul, NSW. She was awarded an Australian Society of Authors Mentorship in 2013–14 to work on her short story collection.

JOSHUA MAULE has worked as a journalist and writes poetry and short stories for leisure. He is studying theology in Sydney.

ANGELA MEYER is the author of a collection of flash fiction, *Captives* (Inkerman & Blunt), editor of *The Great Unknown* (Spineless Wonders), and a literary journalist. literaryminded. com.au

JENNI NIXON is a widely published poet. Her publications include *café boogie* and *agenda!* and her work is included in many anthologies and journals/recently *southerly* and *overland*. She is a member of the company of writers and roundtable writing groups.

A.S. PATRIĆ is the author of *The Rattler & other stories*, *Las Vegas for Vegans* and *Bruno Kramzer.* He has twice featured in *Best Australian Stories* and is the winner of the Ned Kelly Award and Booranga Prize.

DANIEL JOHN PILKINGTON is an emerging writer from Melbourne. He writes poetry, short fiction and aphorisms.

CAROLINE REID's short stories and poems have been published in anthologies and journals. Her plays have been performed and broadcast. *Prayer to an Iron God* was published by Currency Press in 2010.

CHRISTOPHER RINGROSE has lived in Melbourne since 2012. He writes poetry and short fiction, and co-edits the *Journal of Postcolonial Writing* and the Sydney-based fashion magazine *Papier Mâché*. His poetry website is cringrose.com

MARK ROBERTS is a Sydney based writer and critic. He edits *Rochford Street Review* and *P76 Magazine* and is currently Poetry Editor for *Social Alternatives*.

ALLY SCALE has a Master of Arts (Writing and Literature) from Deakin University. Her recent work has been published in *Right Now* and *Ricochet Magazine*. You can follow her latest travels in Iceland at 150daysiniceland.wordpress.com.

CAMERON SEMMENS is a poet, entertainer and poetry educator with many books to his name. He makes his living through writing, workshopping and publishing. He lives in The Dandenongs with his wife and two youngsters.

TIM SINCLAIR is a poet and novelist. His books include *Nine Hours North* (a Japanese travelogue) and *Re:reading the dictionary* (poetry for word nerds). His latest verse novel, *Run*, is a YA paranoid parkour thriller.

ALI JANE SMITH is a poet and critic. Her work has appeared in *Southerly, Cordite, Famous Reporter* and other journals. She is the author of the chapbook *Gala* (Five Islands Press 2006). She lives in Wollongong.

ANGELA SMITH writes poetry and short fiction. Her work has been published widely. She has been awarded several Varuna residencies including a Second Book Fellowship.

MARK SMITH lives, works and surfs on Victoria's West Coast. His stories have appeared in *Visible Ink, Offset, Mascara, Margaret River Press, Spineless Wonders* and *Award Winning Australian Writing,* among others.

JON STEINER studied writing at UTS. His work has been published in the 2007 and 2008 UTS Writers' Anthologies and Spineless Wonders' *Escape* anthology.

KIRSTEN TRANTER is the author of the novels *A Common Loss* and *The Legacy,* and a co-founder of the Stella Prize. She grew up in Sydney and now lives in the San Francisco Bay Area.

BARRIE WALSH, a fruit picker in Griffith NSW, is currently writing a collection of short stories, poems & essays under the working title *Noctural U-Turn Suite* [NUTS]. A few have been published.

IRENE WILKIE's poetry has appeared in many anthologies and journals including *Award Winning Australian Writing* and *Australian Poetry Journal 4.1.* Both her books of poetry, *Love and Galactic Spiders* and *Extravagance* were published by Ginninderra Press.

MICHELLE WRIGHT writes short stories and flash fiction. She's won the Age (2012), Alan Marshall (2014) and Grace Marion Wilson (2013) Awards, and the Writers Victoria Templeberg Fellowship (2013). In 2013, she was placed second in the Bridport Prize for Flash Fiction.

RUTH WYER lives in south-west Sydney. Her stories have won Zinewest 2012, The Margaret River Short Story Competition 2014 and have appeared in *The Sleepers Almanac No. 9*, *The Canary Press* and *Margaret River Press*.

Editors

LINDA GODFREY is an editor, judge and publicist for Spineless Wonders and works as a freelance editor. Her fiction and poetry has appeared in *Cordite*, the UTS writers' anthology *Nine Tenths Below*, other anthologies, audio anthologies by River Road Press and the Spineless Wonders anthology, *Escape*. She has been co-editor for the Spineless Wonders anthologies, *Small Wonder*, *Stoned Crows & other Australian Icons* and *Writing to the Edge*.

BRONWYN MEHAN is the founding publisher of Spineless Wonders. Her short fiction and poetry have been published in *The Age, The Sleepers Almanac, Meanjin, Southerly, Island* and *Best Australian Poems (2012)*. She won The Red Earth Poetry Award in 2011. She now lives in Sydney after spending almost five years in the Northern Territory.

The joanne burns Award

Each year Spineless Wonders auspices an award for the best writing in the forms of prose poem and microfiction in honour of foremost Australian experimental poet, joanne burns. The award is open to people residing in Australia and to Australians living overseas. Finalists chosen by each year's judging panel are offered publication in our annual anthology alongside invited writers.

The *2013 joanne burns Award* was judged by Shady Cosgrove who selected Mark Smith's '10.42 to Sydenham' as the winning entry and Hilary Hewitt's 'happy' and Mark Robert's 'cities that are not Dublin' as runners-up. All three pieces, along with those of other finalists appear in *Writing to the Edge*, edited by Linda Godfrey and Ali Jane Smith.

The *2012 joanne burns Award* was judged by Carol Jenkins who selected Mark O'Flynn's 'under the maw of luna park' as the winning entry and commended Richard Holt's 'bush burial', Trina Denner's 'playing outside', Stu Hatton's 'down south' and Paul Mitchell's 'The Old Man and the Pool'. The winner and finalists all appear in *Stoned Crows & other Australian Icons*, edited by Julie Chevalier and Linda Godfrey.

The inaugural *joanne burns Award* was held in 2011 and was judged by joanne burns who selected Charles D'Anastasi's 'Madame Bovary' as the winning entry and commended Erin

Gough's 'William Shatner vows to save the Great Basin Pocket Mouse' and Clare McHugh's 'Briefly'. All three pieces, along with those of other finalists appear in *small wonder*, edited by Linda Godfrey and Julie Chevalier.

In *2014, the joanne burns Award* was judged by Angela Meyer and Richard Holt who selected Susan McCreery's 'Hold Up' as the winning entry and Kirsten Tranter's 'Turing Test Study Guide' and Mark Smith's 'The Meteorologist's Daughter' as runners up. All three pieces, along with those of other finalists are published in *Flashing the Square*, edited by Linda Godfrey and Bronwyn Mehan.

ABOUT JOANNE BURNS

joanne burns grew up in Sydney's eastern suburbs. She worked as an English teacher in New South Wales, and for a time in London. She has taught creative writing in tertiary institutions, schools and community organisations. Her first collection of poems, *Snatch*, was published in London in 1972. Since then she has published more than a dozen further books of poetry. Her poems have appeared in numerous Australian literary journals, poetry magazines and have been set for study on the Higher School Certificate syllabus. joanne has been particularly concerned with the blurring of the distinctions between poetry and prose in her work, and has written extensively in prose poem/ microfiction forms. She has also written monologues and short futurist fictions and 'farables' (fables/ parables).Her forthcoming collection is *Brush*, (Giramondo Poets, 2014))

Also from

Spineless Wonders

A treasure trove of writing from some of the most innovative practitioners of prose poetry and microfiction in Australia.

KABITA DHARA, EDITOR, READINGS MONTHLY

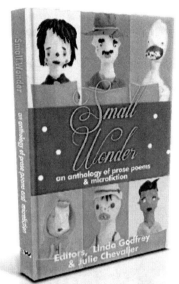

Small Wonder
prose poems & microfiction

edited by Linda Godfrey and Julie Chevalier

Here are short and clever pieces by thirty contemporary Australian writers on the eroticism of mashed potato, parenting as magic realism and a tongue-in-cheek history of the Cyclops bicycle. Includes award-winning writers Michael Farrell, Keri Glastonbury, Judith Beveridge and Peter Boyle. Features prose poems and microfiction selected by competition judge joanne burns.

Illustrated by talented young artist, Paden Hunter.

'Sometimes serious, sometimes humorous, provocative, self-reflective and self-satirising, nostalgic, angry, sad, poetic and personal, realist and stream of consciousness, this collection is above all a celebration of the many things Australia can mean to us.' JEAN BEDFORD, NEWTOWN REVIEW OF BOOKS

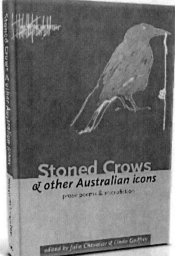

Stoned Crows
& other Australian Icons
prose poems & microfiction

edited by Linda Godfrey and Julie Chevalier

What do our best wordsmiths have to say about Australian icons? This anthology takes a fresh look at everything from the HIH collapse to crocs, Margaret Olley, bush burials and the ABC. We visit a post-apocalyptic Opera House and spend Saturday night in downtown Byron Bay. Tones range from nostalgic to sceptical, from wry to LOL. Featuring prose poems and microfiction by Mark O'Flynn, Anna Kerdijk Nicholson, Michael Sharkey, Moya Costello and many more.

'New voices, new ideas, refreshed old ones and all in degustation morsels to get those creative and imaginative juices flowing. There are terse epigrams full of resonance and affect, gnomish haikus of condensed truth, pithy aphorisms from Melbourne to Marrakesh, from Sydney to Paris.' KATHLEEN MARY FALLON

Writing to the Edge
prose poems & microfiction
edited by Linda Godfrey and Ali Jane Smith

If the art of the short story is knowing what to leave out, what is the art of microfiction? The 33 authors included in *Writing to the Edge* demonstrate many ways of making much from little. In pieces ranging in length from a few pages to a line or two, they intrigue, amuse, sadden and enlighten us in turn. Their carefully chosen words and striking images provide vivid glimpses into other lives, other places, other minds.

Emeritus Professor Elizabeth Webby AM

EARWORMS
short Australian audio

Stories that stay with you

Earworms are those songs with unforgettable hooks that get stuck in your head but Spineless Wonders brings you short Australian earworms—stories by award-winning writers that you definitely won't want to forget.

Stuck in a queue? Don't stress. You can listen to our selection of funny, political and thought-provoking prose poems and microfiction from one of our anthologies. Got a pile of washing-up or ironing to do? Housework's not a chore when you have an audio story.

Commuting every day? Traffic jams are not a problem when you can listen to the latest in contemporary short fiction and microliterature from Spineless Wonders.

Prices range from $0.99 to $2.99. Gift vouchers available.

Listen to our audio trailers now at
www.shortaustralianstories.com.au.

Spineless Wonders publications are available in print and digital format from participating bookshops and online. For further information about where to purchase our print, audio and ebooks, go to the Spineless Wonders website:

www.shortaustralianstories.com.au